PUFFIN BOOKS
THE ASTOUNDINGLY TRUE ADVENTURES OF
DAYDREAMER DEV

Ken Spillman developed his imagination while playing games in bushland on the edge of one of Australia's most isolated cities, and by reading adventures set in faraway places. He is now the author of about eighty books, published in around twenty languages. Ken is a frequent visitor to India and has written a number of books featuring sharp-witted young Indian characters. These include the Daydreamer Dev stories; *Advaita the Writer* (2011); *No Fear, Jiyaa!* (2017); and *Radhika Takes the Plunge* (2012), which was listed in *101 Indian Children's Books We Love!* For more information, visit www.kenspillman.com.

The ASTOUNDINGLY TRUE ADVENTURES of DAYDREAMER DEV

KEN SPILLMAN

ILLUSTRATIONS BY SUVIDHA MISTRY

PUFFIN BOOKS

An imprint of Penguin Random House

PUFFIN BOOKS

USA | Canada | UK | Ireland | Australia
New Zealand | India | South Africa | China

Puffin Books is part of the Penguin Random House group of companies
whose addresses can be found at global.penguinrandomhouse.com

Published by Penguin Random House India Pvt. Ltd
7th Floor, Infinity Tower C, DLF Cyber City,
Gurgaon 122 002, Haryana, India

First published in Puffin Books by Penguin Random House India 2021

Text copyright © Ken Spillman 2021
Illustrations copyright © Suvidha Mistry 2021

ISBN 9780143451761

Typeset in Adobe Caslon Pro by Manipal Technologies Limited, Manipal
Printed at Replika Press Pvt. Ltd, India

www.penguin.co.in

Contents

Contents

DAYDREAMER DEV
BRAVES
A VOLCANO

1

Climbing out of the auto, Amma reminded Dev to focus. To be serious. This, she said, was important. It might be very helpful for him.

'I *will*. I *am*,' Dev told her. 'I *know* it's important.'

Under the shade of an old peepal tree, they made their way to the door. The engraved plate beside it read:

Dr Ira Bharghava
DEVELOPMENTAL PSYCHOLOGIST
ADHD • Learning Difficulties • Autism •
Behavioural Problems

'Wow,' said Dev. 'Dr Bharghava has a lot of problems. But, Amma, why does she want everyone to know?'

Amma refused to smile and rang the bell.

'Don't be silly. Those are some of the areas she specializes in.'

'I thought she specialized around the Fateh Nagar area.'

He wanted Amma to laugh, just once before they went in. It would make him feel better—it

4

always did. But there was a heavy weight on her shoulders and he was the one who had put it there. Why else would they be standing on this particular doorstep at 2.30 p.m. on a school day?

The door swung open and a cheerful young woman ushered them in.

'Dr Ira will be with you soon. Make yourself comfortable while I take some details from your mother,' she instructed Dev.

Amma followed her to the desk. Dev wondered how it was possible to make himself comfortable when he had no idea what the next hour would bring. This was a doctor who might know exactly which part of his brain caused daydreaming. Would she recommend surgery? Electric shocks? Tablets that would make him normal?

School wasn't the place for daydreaming. Dev knew that. He was truly sorry that Mrs Kaur was so concerned that she had asked Amma and Baba to—how had she put it?—'look into it'.

Very shortly, he would walk into Dr Ira's office and she would 'look into it'. Would she see the helicopter that had delivered him to base camp at Mount Everest? Would she see the skin shed by the anaconda that nearly killed him in the Amazon jungle? Would she be fooled by the mirages of the Sahara?[1] And if she found herself flying above the city on a rug specially selected from Kwality Carpets, would she like the view?

---

[1] Editor's note: Dev is thinking about some of his previous adventures, chronicled by the author in *The Absolutely True Adventures of Daydreamer Dev* (Puffin India, 2019).

2

Dr Ira wore dark-rimmed glasses and had a soft, round face and a gentle voice. Dev could imagine her speaking calmly as the *Titanic* went down. She listened carefully to Amma and adjusted her glasses to read the two pages supplied by Dev's headmaster. Dev imagined himself shrinking very steadily so that by the time she looked up, he would be gone.

'Dev, what do you think about all this?'

Dev realized that he must still be visible. 'Ma'am, I think it's very bad that Mrs Kaur needs to write so many notes,' Dev said. 'Amma doesn't like them, and Baba must spend his time lecturing me about concentration and teaching me the meaning of words like "lamentable" and "deplorable".'

'Would you be able to tell me about one of your daydreams, Dev?'

Dev told her about the time he hit a six off the final ball at Wankhede Stadium to win the match against Australia, and about riding on a dolphin. He was launching into another story when she interrupted.

'Do you have some good friends, Dev?'

Surprised that she wanted to talk about his friends, he told her about Vihaan, Adil and the best of friends ever, OP—Omprakash, as only Mrs Kaur preferred to call him.

Dr Ira asked more questions and looked over his school reports. Eventually, she sat back and looked as squarely at Amma as a round-faced woman could manage.

'It would be valuable if I could spend some time with Dev alone on another occasion. Would that be all right, Dev?' Dr Ira paused and when Dev did not say no, she went on. 'Let's be clear— daydreams are normal. But recently, there has been some good research on what is called "maladaptive daydreaming". This is when fantasy tends to take over. And when fantasy takes over, it can get in the way of everyday things, such as education, or the jobs people do.'

Amma was like a sculpture. She was sitting bolt upright with her head tilted and her lips squeezed together.

'Dev seems well adjusted socially,' Dr Ira said. 'And he's managing at school. But Mr Bannerji and the school counsellor believe he is gifted and might do very much better.'

The sculpture beside Dev became Amma again. She nodded vigorously. Dr Ira leant forward.

'I'd like to explore this a little. Maladaptive daydreamers tend to imagine worlds and stories as relief in times of stress or boredom. In Dev's case, I suspect it is boredom. But the ability to daydream so vividly that you experience a sense of presence in an imagined environment can be addictive. I can work with Dev to help him develop some strategies to manage it.'

The word 'maladaptive' came as a relief. Evolution was all about adaptation. Dr Ira probably thought Dev needed to adapt, to evolve. At least he wasn't going to have an operation or an electric shock.

'It will be quite painless, young man,' Dr Ira assured, as if reading his thoughts. 'Think about it like this. Active volcanoes don't erupt every day. In fact, most of them very rarely erupt. Your daydreams can rumble away in the background and that's healthy. We can try to limit unwanted eruptions that affect your education. Does that make sense?'

Actually, it did. And Dev rather liked volcanoes.

3

As the auto puttered homewards, Dev remembered OP talking about a volcano erupting on a small New Zealand island. It was a long while ago now. All he could remember was that some tourists died after coming by boat to take some cool photos.

At the next traffic signal, Dev closed his eyes.

Tuk-tuk-tuk-tuk went the auto.

Tuk-tuk-tuk.

From close behind he heard the sigh of a bus braking and the swish of its doors opening. The engine idled in a lazy rhythmic baritone.

Chug-a . . . chug-a . . . chug-a . . .

Chug-a . . . chug-a . . . chug-a . . .

The boat slowed as it neared its destination. Dev held the railing and gazed across the swell to white-grey cliffs no more than 200 metres away.

The loudspeaker crackled into life.

'Well, good people, the Bay of Plenty has been kind to us today and we've made good time. If you're on our port side, you'll be getting a really beaut look at White Island. That's the name Captain James Cook gave it in 1769, but we prefer our Maori name "Whakaari". If you're not on our port side, get your rear end over there.'

There was laughter all round, but Dev was still trying to make sense of the man's accent. When the man said 'if', it sounded like he'd been punched. *Uff.*

'I know, it's so weird,' said a girl standing beside him.

Dev turned to face her and his jaw dropped. It was Anvi, with a professional-looking camera hanging from a strap round her neck.

'What are you doing here?' Dev asked. He sounded rude but, in that moment, could find no other words.

'The same as you, *duh*. I'm visiting Whakaari.'

Anvi lived on the same street as Dev and their mothers had been friends since he and Anvi were babies. Amma liked to tell Dev how nice Anvi was, conveniently overlooking the fact that she was a girl. Dev couldn't remember actually speaking to Anvi since Class II.

Of all the luck! Why couldn't she be OP?

'What we see is like the tip of an iceberg,' said the guide. 'Whakaari is literally a mountain in the sea. Take away the water and you'd see a volcano 1.6 kilometres high. But the highest point of this island is only 321 metres above sea level—and the crater itself sits only 30 metres above sea level! That makes things easy for us, good people, because you don't need to be a super fit hiker to tick volcanoes off your bucket list!' The guide rattled off more facts and Dev kept his eyes fixed on the island. The air around it shimmered. Steam rising from the middle seemed to shroud it in mystery.

Anvi pointed the camera at him, twisted the lens a few times and clicked a button—but Dev managed to turn away just in time.

'Annoying,' Anvi said.

'I was just about to say the same thing.'

'. . . and as you know, access was prohibited after the tragedy of 2019,' the guide continued.

'Ex-cess was pro-hub-her-tid,' Dev mimicked in a whisper.

Anvi suppressed a smile and shushed him. 'Inappropriate, Dev.'

'. . . permitted to go ashore again. Stay on a track and everything'll be hunky-dory. Now put on those overalls and hard hats and look real fashionable. And don't forget to sling a gas mask round your neck, good people, just in case the atmosphere's too much for you. Go have some fun!'

4

Two rigid inflatables ferried the passengers a short distance to the island. Dev and Anvi were among the last to go. Jagged peaks rose above them, arcing around the crater and the rocky beach in front of them. The breeze was gentle and the swell low, but Dev's hard hat felt wobbly on his head. His nose twitched with irritation.

'It's the gas,' Anvi told him. 'It'll get worse. That's why we've got the gas masks. See all that? The volcano is constantly releasing sulphuric acid.'

Now Dev could see patches of vivid yellow on the incline that led from the beach to the crater.

'A hundred years ago, there was a sulphur mine here,' Anvi added.

Her camera was clicking constantly. A large, red-faced man opposite Dev was holding up his phone in video mode, panning from one peak to another. When he lowered it, he looked at Dev and smiled.

'Yer friend 'ere has ahb-viously done some homework,' he said. He held out his hand. 'Aahm frum Texas.'

Another accent, and again Dev was perplexed for a moment. Arm from Texas? If one arm came from Texas, where had the other arm come from?

'Yes, sir,' he said. 'My name is Dev. I'm from India. She is my neighbour, Anvi.'

'Aahm Rahnie. Y'all remember this, okay? Most folks never get to see stuff near as spectac-lar as this! Me, ah just lerv vahl-caners.'

The man was speaking English, but Dev's ears hadn't yet adjusted to this particular variety of it. *Rahnie,* he repeated to himself. *Ah just lerv vahl-caners.* Suddenly, Dev got it. The man's name was Ronnie, and he was saying that he loved volcanoes.

'Vahl-caners are my ree-al passion. Came here 'bout ten years back and promised mahself I just had to do it agin.'

By now, the inflatable was nearing the shore.

'Why are those rocks so white?' Dev asked.

'It's probably ash,' Anvi told him.

'Maht be,' Ronnie said. His breathing was shallow, like an asthmatic. 'But on this 'ere island, you got gi-normous colonies of gannets. You got gulls, you got petrels, you got terns . . .' He was counting bird families off on his fingers, but couldn't think of any more. 'Anyways, with that many birds, you're gonna get a lot of you-know-what.'

Theek hai, Dev thought. *Remind me to be careful where I step.*

The inflatable beached and, one by one, their little group stepped out. The first thing Dev noticed was that there wasn't a bird in sight. He was opening his mouth to comment when he saw Ronnie, the last to get down, overbalancing as he straddled its rubberized hull. Dev quickly caught hold of his arm. *The arm from Texas*, he thought.

'Now ain't you a fahn young gen-elman,' Ronnie wheezed. 'But you an' your friend jus' run along. Don't be holdin' your horses for an old feller like me.'

Dev shook his head. The immensity of the man's bulk was more obvious now that he was upright. If he needed some help getting down from the inflatable, he might also struggle on the slope.

Anvi must have been thinking the same thing. She had positioned herself on the other side of Ronnie and didn't look in any hurry to 'run along'.

Together, they set off for the crater.

5

From the tour boat, it was easy to see why Captain Cook named the place 'White Island'. Up close, it revealed a secret palette of colours. Sulphur streaked the surface and jutted out in crystalline outcrops. In some places, fine chemical residue gave the illusion of moss, with green and orange hues. Rivulets of pale blue, aqua near the edges, ran across fissures in the rock. 'Stay on a track', the guide had said—now Dev realized that you'd be crazy if you didn't. Even the main track snaked around hot streams and troughs of bubbling mud.

Off to the right, at the foot of a cliff, steam was roaring out of a yellow rock vent.

'That there's called a fumarole,' Ronnie told Dev, gesturing towards the source of the steam. 'And that ain't just water vapour. It's got sulphur dioxide in it, fer starters.' He coughed and wiped his eyes. 'Aahm gonna put on this 'ere mask. But I'll take it off if we're conversin', okay?'

Ronnie looked like a bear now, his gas mask forming a black snout. When he started shooting a video again, Dev fitted his own mask over his face just to try it out. Anvi giggled.

'That's the nicest you've ever looked,' she said, pointing her camera at him.

Dev removed it immediately. The air bit into his nostrils and throat, but it didn't affect his breathing. Once again he wished OP was there.

By now, several groups of tourists had reached the crater. Their guide had been ferried over with the first group, and his red vest made him easy to spot. Dev saw him pointing out some features and felt he was missing out. He kept reminding himself to take small steps beside Ronnie. The big man stopped to catch his breath, stretching the gas mask's elastic to speak.

'This ain't got no easier, that's fer sure.'

As they reached the place where the other tourists had been standing, about half of them turned to follow the guide along a path that disappeared behind a nearby ridge.

'We should follow them,' Anvi said. 'The best views are up high.'

Dev didn't answer. What lay in front of him wasn't a gaping hole, and neither was there any hint of a lava glow from deep inside the belly of the volcano.

It was something else entirely.

6

It was a lake. A steaming, lime-green lake. On the far side of it, the towering crater wall was tinted with huge splashes of yellow and rust red.

Ronnie followed Dev's gaze and held out his mask again. 'See that red? It's aah-ron. Just like the sulphur, it gets thrown up from below.'

Iron, Dev translated. *Got it.*

'Now,' said Ronnie. 'You two gotta stand there. Aahm gonna tek yer picture, just for the memories.' He pulled down his mask and let it hang round his neck.

Anvi had been taking some close-ups of sulphur crystals. 'Just here?'

'Git over there boy. Stand real close.'

Dev didn't want to stand *real* close. *Close* was close enough. And only momentarily.

Ronnie's eyes widened and he lowered his phone. He was looking past them, and Dev and Anvi pivoted in opposite directions, colliding halfway round. Dev jumped back as if girlhood was contagious.

A young man was picking his way down towards the lake.

'That guy's got a death wish,' Ronnie muttered. 'Where's that guide?' He frantically looked around for the man in the red vest.

Dev pointed to the ridge. 'He went up there.'

Ronnie sucked in some of the biting air. 'Don't be no fool,' he shouted. 'You ain't gonna be postin' no selfie if yer fall in.'

The man waved back at Ronnie, dismissing him. He took another step towards the lake.

'Fabio!' A young woman held her head in her hands, her chest heaving. 'Fabio! ¡Vuelve! ¡Es peligroso! Fabio!'

'Maybe he doesn't understand English,' Anvi offered. 'I heard those two on the boat. I think they're Spanish, or from South America.'

Other tourists were shouting to the man now, but he was approaching the edge, holding out his phone and framing his click.

'Jeez,' Ronnie said. 'That ain't no swimmin' pool. It's like battery acid, but it's worse. If he falls in, we're gonna see his skeleton quicker than you can say Jack Robinson.'

Dev had no idea who Jack Robinson was, and he didn't have time to ask.

From deep below came a menacing growl. Anvi screamed. Dev choked as if fear itself had reached out and strangled him.

The lake was bubbling and popping. Before it had looked like hot lime cordial. Now it looked more like moong dal in a pressure cooker.

The man beside it was on all fours. He had dropped his phone, and it was lodged among rocks right on the edge. Putting on his gas mask and shielding his eyes, he reached forward to retrieve it. Another tremor came from far below and the man turned in the direction of the young woman, scrabbling to get up the bank. He moved forward a few metres, his legs such a blur that it made Dev think of Road Runner. But Road Runner never tripped when escaping Wile E. Coyote's traps in the Looney Tunes cartoons. This man dropped like a sack of aloos. He clutched at his ankle helplessly.

'Faaabio!' The woman started gingerly down the slope towards him.

'Don't!' Ronnie bellowed as the lake fired something into the air with a frightening *whoomph*. The lake was going to blow, Dev knew it.

7

Most of the tourists had run for their lives. Dev wanted to join them. He was sure Anvi did too. But how could they? Nearby, a Japanese couple were hesitating as well.

'We gotta help that guy,' Ronnie said.

'Sir . . .' Dev started. 'I have an idea. Anvi, we need more people. Get those two and the Spanish woman.'

Anvi took off without a murmur. *She's braver than I would have imagined*, Dev thought. *Maybe it's the hard hat.*

Fabio was trying to drag himself over loose, jagged rock. From the way he used his hands,

Dev could see that the surface was hot. 'Wait!' he shouted into the crater. 'We're coming to get you.'

Then, remembering that the man may not speak English, Dev showed him the palm of both hands. '*Uno momento!*'

It might have been bad Spanish or bad Italian or bad something else, but the man gave a desperate nod.

As Dev explained his plan to Ronnie, the tour guide appeared, hurrying his little flock of tourists towards the beach. Catching sight of Anvi and the Japanese couple from the corner of his eye, he scanned the scene around the crater.

'You guys! Run for it!'

'Sir,' Dev shouted. 'There's an injured man.'

'Oh hill,' the guide said—or it might have been *hell*. He jogged over to Ronnie. 'Sir, can I help you?'

'Not me, dude. *That* guy.'

Whoomph. Boom. Projectiles shot from the lake like dud pyrotechnics. Smoke mingled with the steamy, acrid air. It was like a war zone.

'Hill, hill, hill,' repeated the guide. 'What the *hill* are we going to do?'

8

'Take your overalls off,' Dev instructed. 'Not you, Ronnie—everyone else. Keep your mask on and just listen. Ronnie, you're going to anchor me.'

Anvi didn't hesitate, quickly unzipping and then tugging the overalls over her shoes. The others looked baffled, and Dev feared they were just going to run to safety.

'Ah, I git it!' the guide exclaimed. 'Like Rapunzel, with clothes instead of hair, right?'

He put his mask on, tore off his red vest and started peeling off his overalls, at the same time

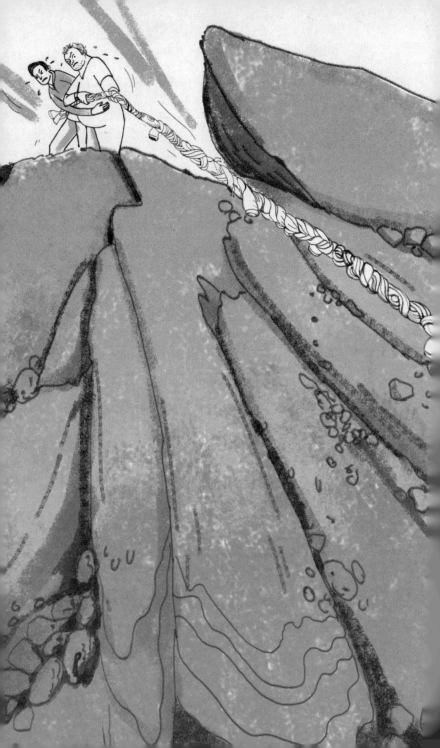

instructing the others in his country's own brand of English.

'You . . . *run*,' the guide urged the Japanese couple when they added their overalls to the pile. '*Run*, okay?'

'O-kay?'

'Okay,' the guide assured.

With the overalls piling up, Dev had started knotting them together—arm to leg, leg to arm. Finally, he tied the first set of legs around Ronnie and the final pair of arms around his own waist. He told the guide to hold on tight to the Texan.

The lake had gone quiet, but it seemed that the whole island was vibrating. Close by, Dev heard the fierce hiss of steam. His face and hands stung as if washed in vinegar. He put on his gas mask, gathered up his makeshift rope and started backing down the incline.

'You GO, boy! You gaht this!' Ronnie had removed his mask and was pumping the air like a fan at a ball game. If he could feel Dev's weight at all, he wasn't showing it.

Fabio was kneeling on one leg, using the opposite elbow to steady himself. Above his mask, his eyes broadcast pain and distress in some universal language. Dev helped him to his feet and turned his back so that Fabio could lean on him and hold on.

With great effort, Dev took one step up the slope. Ronnie and the guide retreated, keeping tension in the link. Dev felt them trying to haul him up, but keeping his footing wasn't easy with the weight of Fabio behind him. With every advance, Dev's calf muscles felt as if they might rip from the bone. It was slow going.

But he got there.

'Faabio, Faaabio,' cried the Spanish woman. '¡Estúpido hombre!'

Estúpido. It wasn't difficult to figure out what that meant. In Dev's state of exhaustion, he could only agree with her.

9

Leaving the pile of overalls at the crater, they made for the track. Ronnie swung his arms vigorously, but it didn't seem to make his legs move faster. Dev and Anvi urged him on, glancing anxiously back at the others, who were falling further and further behind. Fabio had started out hopping, one arm draped over the guide's shoulders, the woman alongside them. Soon the guide was half-dragging, half-carrying him.

The Japanese couple had been whisked across to the tour boat the moment they reached the beach. Now, both inflatables were ashore, waiting. They looked close and Dev knew that a mighty sprint could get him down to them in not much more than a minute.

Not many things are harder than resisting the instinct to survive. Dev knew that every metre he did not run could be the difference between life and death. His heart was thumping, but it wasn't because of his exertions at the crater.

'Anvi, run for it,' he said. 'You can get across to the boat and they'll come back before Ronnie can say Jack What's-his-name.'

'Jack *Robinson*. But you're kidding, right? What you did back there was cool, but I'm not going to let anyone say I deserted you. What would our mothers say if we didn't stick together?'

Boom.

Whoomph, boom, whoomph.

The angry crater had fired up again. Reverberations shook the island. A wide plume of smoke billowed upwards. Ash fell like heavy snow.

Ronnie stopped and pulled away his gas mask. His face was beetroot and dripping with sweat.

'Fer cryin' out loud,' he panted. 'You guys gotta run. Y'got yer whole lives ahead of yer. Aahm an old guy with a heart condition . . .'

Boom.

Piping hot fragments of rock pelted the slope. Anvi grabbed Ronnie's arm and shouted above the din.

'Gas mask back on! Now!'

'Dang it, then,' Ronnie said.

'You too, Dev!'

They did as they were told as Anvi pulled on her own mask. They started forward, with Anvi tugging at Ronnie's hand.

Whoomph, boom. The bombardment continued. A fragment flew past Dev's shoulder. Under his mask, Ronnie swore.

When finally they reached the water, the man at the wheel of the inflatable pulled Ronnie head first over the side. Without waiting for him to sit up, Dev and Anvi jumped in and they sped away. Dev kept his gaze on the island, looking hard through swirls of smoke and steam, trying to pick out the guide and the two remaining tourists.

10

Almost everyone on board was leaning against the railing, riveted by Whakaari's fearsome display of natural forces and the greatest photo opportunity of their lives. News channels would run video of the inflatable carrying the guide and the two Spaniards, leaving a trail of white water as it made its getaway. Ronnie settled into a seat and let out a hefty sigh.

'They're gonna make it. You done good, guys. Ree-al good. That was kinda hair-raisin', weren't it now?'

'I suppose that's why they call it an adventure tour,' Dev replied.

Anvi grinned. 'Such a comedian.'

But the moment the last group came aboard, there was an almighty blast. The volcano pumped a massive column of smoke and ash skywards. To Dev, it seemed like the work of a nuclear weapon. The column darkened at its base—and what he saw next made him gasp. A rush of lava spewed from the crater and rolled rapidly down the slope, covering the track they had followed, sizzling into the waters of the bay.

The skipper gunned the tour boat's engines, racing blindly through the ash cloud until they were well out of range.

With one hand still on the railing, Dev sat down. He was spent. The boat was puttering now, safe in the middle of the Bay of Plenty. Anvi put a lens cap on her camera and delved into the backpack she had left on her seat. Dev let his chin drop to his chest.

'Would you like a Karachi biscuit?'

He hadn't noticed it before, but Anvi's voice was very much like Amma's. His lungs were burning, his throat was sore and his nose was itchy inside.

He shook his head.

'The pollution in this city gets worse every year,' Amma observed. 'We should be wearing masks whenever we step outside.'

She leant over to pay the auto driver and Dev let go of the side rail.

'Chalo,' Amma said.

Anvi was arriving home from school as they crossed to the pavement. Amma called out a greeting and held up her bag.

'Would you like a Karachi biscuit?'

Anvi glanced at Dev, then back at Amma. 'Aunty, I *need* a Karachi biscuit. You couldn't even imagine the day I've had.'

Dev thought that he probably could.

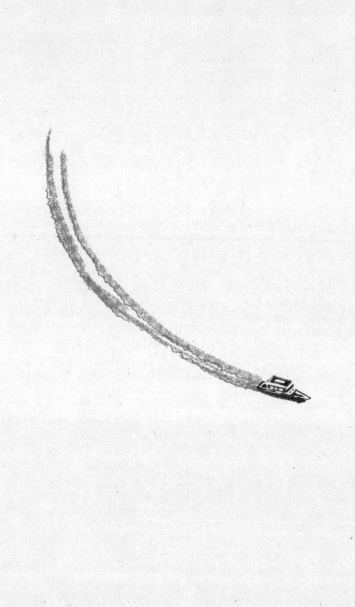

DAYDREAMER DEV

DEV

REACHES

THE SOUTH POLE

1

Dev preferred inspiration to perspiration, but the lunch break had been just what he needed. Hurtling around the football pitch, the weight that landed on his shoulders during maths class had shaken free. Not all of it, of course, but Dev was more than happy to leave one chunk of his worries on the patchy grass for another kid to find. Perhaps, he thought, he might see it in Lost Property sometime.

His shirt was damp with sweat. He leant over, hands on hips, catching his breath.

OP gave him a mighty slap on the back. 'I've never seen you run so much,' he said.

Dev grimaced. 'I usually do my running in daydreams. Night dreams, too.'

'And you are the only person I've seen running around for an entire game without touching the ball. Two players in the EPL have played a game without getting a touch but, to be fair, both were subbed off after the first ten minutes.'

OP was a good friend. The best. He was also like the child of a marriage between the *Ultimate Book of Trivia* and *Encyclopaedia Britannica.* The facts in his head could be useful, but useless information was OP's speciality. Right now, Dev knew that his banter was only intended to help him get his mind off things.

Numeracy-related things, to be precise.

'Don't worry,' OP said, as if reading Dev's mind. 'Lots of other kids had bad results. Yours was only mediocre. It's all relative.'

Relative. It was a relative Dev was worried about—a very close relative too.

When Mrs Kaur returned his test, she had eyeballed him for three eternities. The top of the page in front of him told Dev that her scrutiny was not due to his runny nose. A mark of 59 per cent was even worse than last time, the same last time that had caused both Baba and Amma to call another meeting with the headmaster. Baba's lecture that evening had been a classic. Although delivered to an audience of only one, it would surely have matched the speeches of Tagore, Vivekananda and Nehru for structure and eloquence.

One phrase stuck in Dev's mind. According to Baba, Dev was 'at the brink of the crossroads'.

At the time, this seemed both good and bad. On one hand, it meant that he hadn't reached the crossroads. On the other, it made the crossroads he would soon reach sound like an abyss.

Returning to class, Dev had a feeling that today's result might confirm to Baba that the downfall of his one and only son was both imminent and inevitable.

2

Mrs Kaur seemed sweaty after lunch, too. The staffroom, like Mr Bannerji's office and the front reception area, had top-notch AC and was the envy of all students—Dev included. Mrs Kaur must have spent her break elsewhere. Perhaps, Dev thought, she was training for a marathon.

The fans overhead did their thing: *Pht-pht-pht-pht.* The movement of air on Dev's damp shirt was pleasant, and Mrs Kaur's mention of the Arctic Circle sent a chill through him.

She had been walking back and forth while Dev pondered the unfairness of staffroom cooling and the possibility that he might one day turn on the

TV to see his teacher winning the Commonwealth Games marathon. He inspected her shoes as she turned to him.

'So how, do you think, does the melting of the ice affect climate change?'

'Ma'am,' began Dev, 'it is the opposite. Climate change causes the ice to melt.'

'Just as I suspected—you have not been one hundred per cent tuned in. Right, Dev?'

'Maybe 98 per cent, ma'am.'

'Ninety-eight per cent daydreaming would be more accurate,' Mrs Kaur replied. Now, we have just said that scientists record ice coverage at its *minimum* each year, and that minimum Arctic ice has *declined* by 12 per cent every decade since 1980.' She paused dramatically, as if repeating this information was more exhausting than marathon running. 'Now think, Dev, what is the connection between this and the fact that our average temperatures could rise by 5 per cent during your lifetime?'

Around Dev, several students raised their hands, eager to show Mrs Kaur their grasp of climate science. OP showed his loyalty to Dev by crossing his arms to prevent one of them from shooting upwards.

'Well, Dev?'

Dev was flummoxed. Melting ice would surely mean cooler oceans. Cooler oceans would mean cooler breezes across land. Temperatures should go down, no?

Thankfully, Mrs Kaur had momentarily lost interest in him.

'Yes, Sara?'

Sara puffed out her puny chest. 'Ma'am, ice reflects most of the sun's rays, while the sea absorbs most of the sun's rays. If there is less Arctic ice to reflect the sun's rays, the planet becomes warmer.'

'Correct,' Mrs Kaur said. She turned in Dev's direction as if to say, 'Got that?'

Dev did get it, kind of. He pictured an Arctic Circle without ice, with seaside resorts around the

coastlines of Canada, Russia, Greenland and some of those Scandinavian countries. But a question was forming in his mind.

'What about Antarctica?' he blurted.

'Yes, Dev?'

'Excuse me, ma'am,' Dev corrected, 'but what is happening at the South Pole?'

'Good question! Everyone will be required to present an assignment on climate change and the Arctic. But since you are so interested, Dev, perhaps you could find out about the *Antarctic* for us?' Mrs Kaur smiled. 'We'd like that, wouldn't we, class?'

Not for the first time, Dev wished he had kept his mouth shut.

3

That night, as Dev lay back on the roof of Kwality Carpets, he wondered how long he could delay telling Baba about the maths test.

'Mrs Kaur has not marked them yet,' he had said over dinner. Dev didn't like to lie, but some truths were best told one minute before Baba needed to go somewhere. 'I think she's busy training for a marathon.'

'Now *that* I'd like to see,' Amma had chuckled. 'What an imagination you have!'

Baba cracked a popadum and bit into it. 'Next,'—*crunch, crunch*—'you'll be telling us that

Mr Bannerji'—*crunch, crunch*—'is challenging the world heavyweight boxing champion.'

Dev thought that would be cool. *Very* cool.

Not as cool as the Antarctic, though, which was now challenging maths for the title of Dev's Heavyweight Problem. It would have been so much easier to compare notes on the Arctic with everybody else.

Gazing at the glow of a single star visible through the smog-filled sky, Dev realized that the only thing he knew about the South Pole was that it was the southern hemisphere's version of the North Pole. He had sometimes heard people say 'polar opposites', but hadn't given much thought to the phrase. And while the poles were literally poles apart, he pictured them as twins, identical in their whiteness and coldness. Identical in their remoteness from Kwality Carpets, too, and Mrs Kaur's assignments, and life as he knew it.

The November night was a fraction chilly. Dev wasn't sure whether that fraction was three quarters or seven eighths, which might explain why maths tests were so, well, *testing* for him.

He sat up and pulled on the windcheater he had been using as a pillow.

The first small movement under him was almost imperceptible, but the next was like the restlessness of a saddled-up horse. When his favourite old rug curled at the tasselled edge in front of him, Dev knew it had plans.

He guessed they were heading south.

4

Below Dev was an icy airstrip and a neat town of tents, most of them with the appearance of half-buried balloons. A few rectangular dongas and a motley fleet of vehicles gave the little settlement an entrenched look, and made Dev wonder whether its inhabitants were Antarctica's natives.

He skidded to a halt at the feet of a man wearing a fleecy hood. He was carrying an oilcan.

'Well, if it isn't Aladdin and his magic carpet,' said the man, shaking his head.

'Are you an Eskimo?' Dev asked. He rolled up his rug and stood up.

'Er, no—I'm a mechanic.' The voice came from the depths of a bushy beard. The man had his eyes

on the rug, clearly fascinated. 'And you wouldn't be needing no mechanic, not with that little wonder.'

'You're not an Eskimo?'

'I'm from the States,' the beard informed him in a matter-of-fact way. 'And, by the way, that word "Eskimo" can cause offence. "Inuit" is better. But if yer looking for Inuit people, yer in the wrong place. Yer thinking of the Arctic. This is the *Ant*-arctic.'

Dev was a little fazed the realization that he was clueless about Eskimos—OP would have known that they were picky about poles—but he tried not to show it.

'Ah, so this is the South Pole. I think my little rug may need a new GPS.'

'Not *exactly* the South Pole. Yer've got yerself to a place called Union Glacier. But there's a tour group leaving fer eighty nine degrees south in ten minutes, if ye'd like to join 'em.'

So, Dev thought, *89°S*. He had learnt that the North Pole was at 90°N, so it seemed safe to assume that the South Pole was at 90°S. And since 89 came just before 90, the man's proposal sounded good.

'Count me in,' he said, shivering.

5

Dev was expecting to join the tourists in one of the SUVs he had seen, or in a convoy of snowmobiles or possibly on one of the broad-tyred bicycles someone was riding. Instead, he was led to the airstrip. There were two aeroplanes on the ice, the smaller one resting on skis. Two men were loading boat-shaped sleds into its hold, and the mechanic nodded to them as he left Dev with a cluster of people in heavy jackets waiting to board.

Dev was freezing, even wearing his trusty windcheater. *November*, he thought, *almost winter*.

'I only wish I came in summer,' he said to no one in particular.

A young woman looked him up and down. 'Goodness, look at what you're wearing!'

'Technically, you did come in summer,' the man beside her told Dev.

'Really?'

'Summer here runs from October through to February. And one of the guys told me that this is the nicest day they've had for a while, so you're kind of lucky. It's almost ten degrees below.'

'Below zero?'

'Right,' said the man. 'Are you looking forward to the trek?'

Before Dev had time to consider what this question might mean, the group was ushered on board. Still clutching his rug, he took a seat near a window, just in front of the couple he had been speaking to. A guide came down the aisle collecting ticket stubs.

'Sorry, I'm a late arrival,' Dev told her. 'Mrs Kaur wants me to write something about Antarctica.'

The guide gaped at him. 'Do you realize these people have paid fifty thousand dollars for this experience?'

'O-o-kayy. And what is the cost for children?'

The guide leant towards him and lowered her voice. Obviously, she didn't want to make a scene.

'Actually, we don't have a price for children.'

'Awesome!' Dev exclaimed. 'Most considerate. I simply cannot wait to tell OP that I've seen the South Pole!'

6

Once in the air, the guide regained her composure and seemed to take pity on Dev. Now she sat beside him, explaining that 89°S was 99 miles from 90°S, and that the tourists on board were going to haul sleds for five days before they reached their destination.

Dev couldn't believe it. Fifty thousand dollars and the tour company wouldn't even take them all the way? Sixty-nine miles. Dev wasn't sure how many kilometres that was, but he figured it was more than a hundred.

No way. He didn't need to prove his physical endurance—not again, not right now.

His priority was to find out about the ice cap and global warming.

'I am grateful to you for explaining everything, but may I ask you for a favour?'

'Sure,' the guide smiled indulgently. 'And I think I know what it is. *Of course* we'll fly you back to Union. It's the only sensible thing to do.'

'In fact, I want to ask two favours, and that is not one of them.'

The guide shifted in her seat, giving him her full attention.

'I have saved 265 rupees. I can send you 250 rupees in cash if you fly me all the way to the South Pole.'

'Hmm.'

'And after that, I would like to meet someone who knows a lot about climate change.'

'I see.'

The guide sat back, her eyes now fixed on the cabin ceiling. Dev held his tongue, careful not to push his luck any further.

Just when the silence was becoming uncomfortable, he felt a tap on his shoulder. It was the man behind him.

'I couldn't help overhearing,' he said. 'I can't help you *reach* the South Pole, but back home in Australia, I'm a schoolteacher. My classes study Antarctica every year.'

Dev's eyes lit up. 'Thank you, sir. It would be most helpful if you could tell me where they go.'

'Google,' the man replied. 'Just search up the Australian Antarctic Program. They've had scientists here for over seventy years.'

Seriously? Dev thought. *After seventy years, isn't it time those poor scientists were allowed to retire?*

7

After a brief conference with the pilot, the guide came back beaming.

'Good news. We've got clearance to land at Paulus after we leave 89°S. Then we can fly you to Mawson.'

'Excuse me . . . Paulus? What's that?'

'The aerodrome right at the pole.'

'You're the best! Thank you. And what is Mawson?'

'It's what your Australian friend was talking about. Antarctica's oldest research station. After Mawson, it's up to you.' She stood to leave and,

as if by some prearranged plan, the man behind Dev took her place.

'Once a teacher, always a teacher,' he said. 'If you're going to Mawson, I'd better clue you in on some basics.'

For the remainder of the flight to 89°S, the man didn't stop firing questions—and then supplying the answers.

'What's the main difference between the Arctic and the Antarctic?'

'Er . . . one is north, the other is sou—'

'The Arctic is an ocean. The Antarctic is a continent. So, which one has more ice?'

The answer to that one seemed obvious. 'The Arctic.'

'The Antarctic. It has 90 per cent of the world's ice and 80 per cent of the world's fresh water.'

Dev was glad that the teacher questioning him was not named Mrs Kaur.

'Approximately how many polar bears would you find here?'

Polar bears were an endangered species—everyone knew that. 'Well, less than there were ten years ago . . .'

'Wrong,' said the man. 'Exactly the *same* number as it was ten years ago. Zero! Antarctica has penguins galore. And heaps of seals. But no polar bears, ever.'

That gave Dev an idea. If polar bears were endangered in the Arctic, why not move some of them south? Kind of like the story of Noah's ark, except that all the other kinds of animals would miss out on invitations. He didn't have time to voice his idea before the man's next question.

'Who owns Antarctica?'

Trick question, thought Dev. *Not Eskimos.* 'The original inhabita—'

'No,' the man broke in. 'Antarctica is the only continent that doesn't have a native population. And there's an international treaty that says no nation can ever own it. It's politically neutral and can only be used for peaceful purposes. Any questions?'

'Yes, sir. With you as their teacher, why do your students need Google?'

8

'So that is it?'

Dev wondered why the pilot and the guide hadn't just shown him a photo. He could have saved them the bother of landing. He felt sorry for the people who had disembarked at 89°S if this was all they would get to see after a long trek.

The actual pole at the South Pole would not rank among the seven *lakh* wonders of the world. Fancier poles were erected at the entrance of every Indian wedding. This one was no taller than Dev, and it looked like a half-eaten candy cane with a mirrorball on top. Perhaps, he thought, the people in charge of poles had spent all their money at the North Pole—after all, that one was anchored in an ocean.

Back in the sky again, Dev could hardly keep his eyes open. He fought sleep valiantly but lost. Somehow, he also lost an aeroplane, a pilot and a very helpful guide. When he awoke, he stood before an ultra-modern building on V-shaped stilts.

'What brings you here, young fella?'

Dev swung around to see a big man and a much shorter woman, both wearing wrap-around sunglasses. The man's oversized yellow jacket and his beanie had 'Australian Antarctic Program' printed around the perimeter of an embroidered logo.

'Sir, is this Mawson?' Dev asked. He pinned his rug under his left armpit and stepped forward to shake hands.

'No,' the man said. 'It's Bharati.'

'Bharati?'

Dev wasn't sure whether he had misheard. Perhaps the man had guessed he was from India. Was he joking?

'I do work at Mawson, but I've been visiting Jaya here. India currently has two research stations in Antarctica, and this is one of them. Sometimes, we exchange notes—all in the name of science.'

'Then it is my lucky day. I'm from India, and I am researching Antarctica. May I have your good name?'

'Call me Mike. I've been called worse names, so Mike must be a good one.'

'I am Dev.'

The woman pulled away her sunglasses and eyed Dev with astonishment.

'Dev? The famous Daydreamer Dev? I have read so much about you! Your conquest of Everest, your Amazon adventures . . . What an incredible honour it is to meet you!'

It was Dev's turn to be astonished. He had no idea that his restless mind had brought him such fame.

'Sir . . . ma'am . . . I need to know about the effect of climate change here.'

The man hooted. 'So do I! That's why both our countries have got people studying it!'

'I'm hoping you can tell me something about it . . . Mrs Kaur, you see . . .'

9

Jaya was a seismologist.

'You study earthquakes, ma'am?' Dev asked.

'Seismologists do study earthquakes, yes. But my interest is tectonics.' Dev's blank expression prompted her to go on. 'It all started with Gondwanaland. Millions of years ago, this part of Antarctica was joined to India and—'

'Dev,' Mike broke in, 'I need to get back to Mawson.' He gestured towards a heliport and a chopper bearing the same logo as his jacket. 'Jaya might be a seismologist, but she knows more than enough about climate change to satisfy your Mrs Kaur.'

'Come, Dev,' Jaya said. 'You look cold and you must be hungry. I'll explain everything inside.'

The interior of the building was even more impressive than its exterior. Jaya led Dev into a room that could easily have been mistaken for the lobby of a fancy hotel.

'It's nice, no?'

'Yes, ma'am. I did not expect such luxury.'

'Then you will be surprised to know that all this has been built from shipping containers. One hundred and thirty-four of them, to be precise.'

Dev made a mental note. When he'd tell OP about this experience, the details would matter. He settled into a large reclining chair and waited while Jaya went off to get some snacks. To Dev's surprise, she returned with a plate of Parle-G, some Haldiram's snacks and a bottle of Sprite.

Did scientists here send shopping lists back to India?

He was about to ask, but Jaya was already showing him numbers, graphs and maps on the screen of her laptop. Her favourite word, it seemed, was 'trending'. One thing was trending up, another was trending down.

Jaya told Dev that because Antarctica is so large, the effects of warming differed from place to place. The western part of the continent was increasing in temperature ten times faster than the rest of the world. Overall, things were not trending very well at all.

'Look at this graph, Dev. This is now. This is five years from now. And that is ten,' she said, pointing at one part of the screen and then another.

Dev saw how rapid the changes really were.

'There are politicians and even leaders, Dev, who want us to believe that climate change isn't real,' she said. 'Those people are not scientists. Vast ice shelves stretch out from Antarctica into the sea, and we know that this sea ice is breaking up. That has not yet affected sea levels very much, but the glaciers are next in line. Increased flow from the glaciers would mean entire islands disappearing. Coastal cities and agricultural land will be swamped.'

'Sounds bad, ma'am.'

'Very bad . . . And more people will be affected in Asia than anywhere else. Food production will fall. Shortages will occur.'

'So that is the bad news. Is there any good news?'

'You want some good news?'

'Yes, please.'

'India won the first Test match against Pakistan.'

10

When Dev awoke, he could not remember coming down from the roof and climbing into bed. He pulled the blanket tight around his body and ran his tongue around his gums, searching for any residue of Jaya's snacks. There was nothing, but he remembered every word she had said.

India and the drift of continents that separated it from Antarctica.

The loss of sea ice due to climate change.

The importance of the glaciers, and all the disasters that would occur if they were to melt.

The need for world leaders to listen to scientists, to do the calculations and face the unpleasant truth.

Dev's stomach tightened. Calculations. Mathematics.

Right now, the truth that Dev needed to face was the lie he had told last night. He told himself that he would confess over breakfast. But Dev realized another truth, too. He not only needed to do better in maths—he wanted to. As Jaya had shown, there was important work to be done with numbers.

He found his father reading the sports section of the *Times of India*. There was a picture of the Indian captain in full flight, driving the ball through the covers.

'Baba, I would like a tutor for maths,' Dev began.

His father looked up. 'We will be talking about this later,' he said. 'First, let's see.'

Baba slurped his tulsi tea. Dev wondered what they would see, and whether they would see the same way forward after first eyeballing the ugliness of his maths result.

'I need to tell you something,' he said.

'I told you, we will see.'

Reading the newspaper didn't make his father deaf, but Dev knew that if Baba had earmuffs, he would use them.

Amma, however, had the hearing of an elephant.

She called out from the wicker daybed. 'What is it you need to tell, beta?'

'Last night, I . . .'

'Yes?'

'I . . .'

'What is it, for goodness' sake?'

'I was cold, Amma. Very cold. I think I will need an extra blanket.'

DAYDREAMER DEV

DEV

VISITS THE MOON

1

No matter what Baba said, Dev could not imagine a life without daydreaming. Even Baba himself must daydream. Why could he not admit it?

As Dev brushed his teeth and combed his hair, he replayed Baba's breakfast oration in his mind.

'O-ho beta! You will not find *me* on one of your drifty-off, floaty-around, catch-me-if-you-can joyrides. From a very young age, I knew exactly where my mind was supposed to be. And that is exactly where I put it. I only wanted to make your dadi proud. Success is not handed to you on a plate or even in a tiffin box while you go off swanning about heaven knows where. I had to go after it with *diligence*.' With that, Baba had sat back and spread his arms wide, embracing the dining room, embracing all their rooms, embracing Kwality Carpets downstairs, the root of all they possessed above it. 'And here we are . . .'

How could that be true? When hours passed without a single customer stepping through the bell-rigged door of Kwality Carpets, the treasured calculator idle in front of him, what thoughts swam through Baba's mind? Accounts, supplies, insurance? His theoretically brilliant but wilful underachiever of a son?

Dev knew that it would be best if he could confine his daydreaming—perhaps by having one special place for it. The roof of Kwality Carpets would be the first choice. There, he could gaze into the clouds and let them wrap him in a cocoon. There, he could take one of Baba's carpets and fly off to other worlds. Outside, traffic had swept fine dust into the morning air.

Dev smiled as he saw OP waiting for him at the corner.

2

'What is the name of the first man in space?'
It crossed Dev's mind to mimic Mrs Kaur. *Omprakash, that is no way to greet someone. Now, let's start again.*

But in OP's world of facts, figures and unceasing wonderment at all that had ever happened on Mother Earth, this was a conversation starter. On another day, he might simply have started reeling off a long list of astronauts, or Nobel Prize winners or statistics from the Indian Premier League.

'Yuri Gagarin,' Dev said. 'You've asked me that before.'

'The first woman?'

That was more difficult. 'Hmm . . .' Dev began. 'I know she was American . . . No, just tell me.'

'Sally Ride. And who was the first Indian?

'Too easy. Rakesh Sharma.'

'The first Indian woman?'

Dev had written an essay on this subject for Mrs Kaur. 'Even easier! Kalpana Chawla.'

They had reached the main intersection. Waiting for the lights to change, OP told Dev what was obvious already—that he had spent last night reading up on space exploration.

'The first three men to walk on the lunar surface were all aged thirty-nine. Even now, after nine more men have walked on the moon, the average age remains thirty-nine. Amazing, no?'

'Why so old?'

'It is probably the ideal age. The scientists must have worked it out. Scientists can work out anything.'

No way. Baba was not much older than thirty-nine, and anybody could see that he was past his prime. Nearly thirty years past his prime, in Dev's humble opinion.

By the time Dev and OP walked through the school gates, Dev could see the future of moon exploration very clearly. Thirty-nine! No wonder moon exploration was progressing so slowly.

What they needed was what the cricket commentators always talked about.

An injection of youth.

3

'You are just what the moon needs, young fellow,' the man near the hatch said. 'An injection of youth.'

He was clearly British, but the man beside him looked Indian. Dev wasn't sure how old they might be. Not thirty-nine, surely? No, closer to twenty-nine. Not even close to Baba's age. These guys looked capable of tying up their shoelaces without huffing and puffing.

'Yes, sir, but I've been there before, sir. It isn't on the official records because I travelled on a nice blue rug from Kwality Carpets. I landed softly and

gazed back at this planet for the entire duration of a science class.'

'Excellent,' said the Indian man, though he didn't sound convinced. 'My name is Venkatesh, but you must call me Venky. Our English colleague's name is Owen, but for some strange reason he likes to be called Bunny.'

'Sir, I am Dev, and you may call me . . .' *Should I make something up?* Dev wondered. *Is that the big thing on these missions?* 'You may call me whatever you like.'

'Excellent,' Venky said again. 'But Whatever-You-Like is long, so we will persist with Dev.'

Bunny rolled his eyes. 'You better get used to bad jokes,' he said. 'Or it's going to be a long journey.'

Venky chuckled. 'Not so long. Only to the moon and back. Let us tell you more.'

As Dev suspected, this wasn't the latest Chandrayaan.

'We are working for a consortium,' Venky said.

OP would know what a consortium was, but Dev could only imagine. It sounded like something radioactive.

Bunny sensed his confusion. 'The consortium is a group of some of the major tech, mining and innovation corporations in the world. British, Indian, Korean and Australian. We have several goals, but to sum it all up, we're part of a programme that will one day see resources on the moon being used here on Earth.'

'An export base,' Venky said.

'Cool.'

'After touching down, we're going to split up. There will be five of us, with five foldable LRVs . . .'

'Lunar Roving Vehicles,' Bunny broke in.

'. . . and we'll distribute robots carrying thermal sensing cameras. Understand?'

Dev nodded. *Easier than remembering the name of Sally Ride*, he thought.

Venky beamed. 'Excellent!'

4

'All aboard?'

It was the Australian woman, whose name was Uma. She was joking. This wasn't an interstate express train.

'Ma'am, isn't Uma an Indian name?' Dev had asked when they were introduced.

'It is, and it isn't, and don't call me ma'am. My mother's family comes from Bosnia. There are Umas in that part of the world as well.'

The five of them were strapped in. Dev, Bunny, Venky, Uma and a Korean woman named Min Hyo Rin—Rinny, as the others called her.

'If anyone is not on board yet,' Venky said, 'it is too late.'

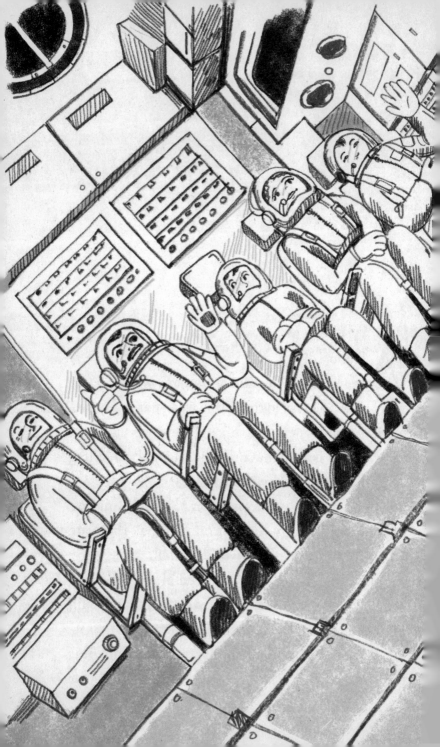

He was right. The monitor in front of them—above them, in fact, since they were all facing skywards—showed the number '56' and seconds were ticking away. The SRBs—Solid Rocket Boosters, Bunny had explained—were fired up and only earphones enabled the astronauts to hear each other.

28 . . . 27 . . . 26 . . .

'On Qantas Airways, we'd be munching nuts by now,' Uma mused.

'Excellent,' said Venky, sounding a little nervous.

14 . . . 13 . . . 12 . . . 11 . . .

'Why time so srow?' This was Rinny. 'Ten second rike ten minute!'

5 . . . 4 . . . 3 . . . 2 . . .

The SRBs unleashed their full fury. Dev had no sensation of movement—only shock. It was as if someone massive had kicked him. The clouds were behind them in an instant.

A carpet ride wasn't like this at all. The monitor told Dev that he was travelling at 28,000 kilometres per hour, and it seemed to Dev that his stomach and all that was left of his breakfast had inconveniently decided to stay earthbound.

Once the worst of this feeling had passed, Dev allowed himself to be swallowed up by the endlessness before him. As Rinny had observed, time itself seemed to have mutated. Was it only two minutes later that the SRBs detached themselves from the spaceship? In their absence, a kind of peace came over the cabin.

'Phase one accomplished,' Rinny announced cheerfully. 'Now for the ET.'

Extraterrestrials? Dev thought.

He turned to look at her. 'Ma'am, are you kidding me?'

Uma cackled but said nothing.

'ET is how we refer to the External Tank,' Bunny told Dev. 'Once the propellant is used up, the ET is let go from the orbiter as well.'

'Orbiter?'

'That's what we're sitting in.'

Why couldn't these people speak plain English? Dev was tempted to ask whether they had ever heard of PE and SWA.

'PE? SWA?' Venky might ask. 'What are those?'

'Plain English and Speech Without Abbreviations.'

But Dev kept silent and waited for the ET separation. Very soon, it happened.

'Phase two accomprished,' said Rinny. 'Time to rerax, everybody.' She released the fasteners on her seat and floated upwards, like a scuba diver in the deep sea. Uma did the same.

Dev could hardly believe it. Not much more than ten minutes after blast-off, he was in space, orbiting Earth.

This was SO epic. But Dev knew that the biggest adventure lay ahead.

5

Bunny was taking a nap. Venky was communicating with the Mission Control Centre, predictably referred to as MCC. Dev joined Rinny and Uma in the game of floating around the cabin, but as soon as the initial thrill passed, he began feeling unwell. If he hadn't left his stomach back on Earth, he would probably have emptied it.

'Is there such a thing as space sickness?' he asked.

'It's called SAS, bro,' Uma said.

'Space Adaptation Syndrome,' Rinny translated. 'Cause by weightressness. Sometimes, it is possiber

for even trained astronauts to experience SAS, even after many rong hours of training.'

Uma giggled. 'Or even right hours.'

'You be quiet, girrfrien,' Rinny told her. 'You Austrarian have accent rike nuffing on earf.'

'Does that make my accent extraterrestrial?' Uma laughed again.

It seemed to Dev that these two weren't showing much sympathy for him. He returned to his seat and hoped SAS might soon become SCS—Space Comfort Syndrome. His thoughts turned to the prospect of zooming around on a foldable vehicle, setting robots free and exploring the lunar surface on his own. The only thing better, he reflected, might be exploring it with OP.

Suddenly, Dev caught a gobsmacking glimpse of home—a sphere more radiant than the globe that sat on a low table in the school library, and far more beautiful than any image of it on the Internet.

Earth—the blue planet. A blanket of cloud hung over Central Asia, but the subcontinent was defined like the flipper of a turtle. Through one small window he could see the nation, and beyond that, the world. He may have gazed upon this

spectacle before, but it made no difference. The sight took his breath away—yet at the same time filled him up.

Just then, Bunny woke up and moved closer to the monitor.

'Oh blimey,' he muttered. 'Venky, Rinny, look.'

Venky had fallen into the same swoon that Dev experienced on seeing India laid out in all her magnificence.

A short, boxed message had appeared in one corner of the screen, no bigger than a calendar alert on Amma's phone.

'Come on, guys,' said Uma, using her hands to pull herself forward on the ceiling. She hadn't put her feet on the floor since they had entered the orbit. 'Cut the suspense. What's up?'

Bunny, Venky and Rinny were moving through drop-down menus on the screen, only stopping when they came to a heavy bank of data.

'What do you wan? Good news or bad news?' Rinny asked.

'I can already see what the bad news is,' Bunny said. 'It's a vent. What's the good news?'

Rinny smiled. 'A rittle EVA can fix that vent. No probrem.'

'Excellent,' Venky said.

6

EVA turned out to mean Extra Vehicular Activity. And Extra Vehicular Activity turned out to mean this: *getting out of the spaceship.*

'Not all of us,' Bunny explained. 'Just Rinny. She's our expert on vents.'

Dev would never have guessed that vents existed on a spaceship, and he couldn't help saying so.

Bunny nodded. 'It's complex, Dev. Up here, we recycle water. We also use water to create oxygen. But, as you know, water contains hydrogen as well as oxygen. We combine that hydrogen with the carbon dioxide we breathe out to produce more water and a by-product is methane. We don't want methane, so we blow it out through special vents.'

'Sir, where is your lab?' Dev wanted to watch the process—that way he might understand it.

'Everything's automated,' Bunny said.

Rinny returned from the back of the spacecraft dressed in a spacesuit that doubled her size.

'You're actually going out there, ma'am?'

'I am actuary going out . . .'

'May I come and watch?'

'OMG!' Uma cried. 'You rock, kiddo!'

'Now listen,' Venky said. 'EVA is not a doddle . . .'

'I know. When I flew into space on my carpet, I . . .'

'As rong as you don't get in my way,' Rinny decided.

With that, Bunny helped Dev towards the back of the spaceship and helped him into his suit, explaining each of its parts. The first layer was for cooling and ventilation. Over this went a combination of hard shell and layered fabric, with so many hidden compartments that Dev lost track of them. The part that really caught his interest was called SAFER. This stood for Simplified Aid for EVA Rescue, and it was what any normal person would call a jetpack. Dev couldn't wait to use it.

'Sorry,' Bunny said. 'It's only for emergencies—like getting separated from the ship.'

'I'll keep that in mind,' Dev replied, keen to arrange a separation. 'Show me how it works.'

Bunny was still explaining SAFER to Dev when they went back to the others.

Venky wasn't sure about Rinny's decision to let Dev tag along. 'Even if one accepts your claim about experience gained through your operation of the goods of Kwality Carpets, I cannot help thinking that your amma would not approve.'

'Sir, I have a question. Does your amma worry about you?'

Venky smiled. '*Haan*. But . . .'

'Game, set and match,' said Uma. She turned to Rinny. 'Now girl, tethers.'

Uma attached one end of a thick cord to Dev's spacesuit, and the other to Rinny's. She then attached longer cords to them, leaving the other end loose, and helped them through an airlock door.

'Have fun, guys!'

Dev and Rinny were now in a small chamber. Rinny locked the internal door, checked it and hitched the loose ends of the cords to shackles near the other door.

'Forrow me,' she said.

Stepping outside was like stepping into nothingness. Sitting on a rug flying high above the city or looking across the Himalayas from the summit of Everest didn't compare. Even bound by a couple of tethers, this was freedom.

Dev forgot all about his jetpack. Orbiting Earth in just a spacesuit, with a spaceship alongside him and all the problems of the world reduced to the size of a marble?

Unforgettable.

7

Rinny proved every bit the expert that Bunny had said she was. Dev's spacewalk ended too soon, and he felt the sting of disappointment as they returned to the chamber and shut the external door.

With the vent fixed and their path aligning with that of the moon, Bunny announced, it was time to get busy.

'Excellent,' Venky said. 'Buckle up, Dev. We're going into phase three.'

Uma settled into the seat beside Dev and explained that only a little engine power was required to change course. Then she lowered her voice. 'Listen, do you want to know why we're really here?'

'Bunny and Venky told me—it's about robots looking for minerals we can use on Earth.'

'Yes, bro! But the consortium is most interested in lithium. Demand for lithium is skyrocketing.' Saying this, Uma paused and giggled. 'And a lot of the lithium we have on Earth is hard to get.'

'So the moon is easier?'

Dev thought he was being funny, but Uma nodded. 'Exactly. And the moon has oodles of it. With lithium being used for batteries, glass, rocket fuel and lasers, a mine here would be worth a . . .'

She stopped and glanced upwards. Dev followed her gaze.

The others looked too.

Rinny's mouth fell open.

'Holy mackerel!' Bunny bellowed.

'*Arey baap re*,' Venky whispered.

OP's scuffed shoes were dangling beside Uma's head. OP was in his school uniform, both hands on a railing so that he could hover in one place.

'Sorry about this,' OP said, 'but I have had enough of being stowed. I am only half hearing so

many interesting conversations. You were talking about lithium, no?'

'This is my classmate, Omprakash, and believe me—I had no idea he was on board. Everyone calls him OP.'

'Excellent,' Venky said, looking dazed.

8

'Oh, it was not hard at all,' OP explained. 'It did not take much deduction to know where you were going, so I followed. If Alan Shepard could smuggle golf balls on to Apollo 14, I knew I could get aboard somehow. I climbed into one of the boxes they were loading on board and ended up alongside a robot. Not the most talkative companion, I must say.'

OP seemed to fit right in. Dev wondered whether having initials for a name helped. Knowing this crew, it probably did.

Landing on the moon was just as Dev remembered it—soft.

Unloading boxes that would be far too heavy for him on Earth was fun. 'I'm the world's strongest man,' he told OP, holding one handle of a fifty-kilo box with his little finger.

That set OP off. 'Between 2002 and 2009, a Polish man named Pudzianowski won the title of World's Strongest Man five times. He came second twice.'

Sometimes, Dev knew, his friend couldn't see beyond the mishmash of trivia that filled every fold of his brain. Dev didn't have that problem, and what he saw right now was four astronauts unpacking various contraptions from the boxes.

'Those must be the LRVs,' he said, seeing Uma unfold a three-wheeler.

'LRVs?' The voice from inside OP's spacesuit didn't sound like OP at all.

'You mean OP doesn't know what an LRV is? The encyclopaedia himself? It means Lunar Roving Vehicle.'

'Oh . . . right. That looks like an autorickshaw without its roof. And for your information, LRV can also stand for Light Reflectance Value and . . .' He stopped mid-sentence, gesturing towards

Venky and Rinny. They were attaching solar panels to rather basic-looking cylinders fitted with four spidery legs. 'Those are the robots,' he told Dev. 'I figured that out while cramped up as the first space stowaway in history.'

'What about me? I got here too.'

'But you were not stowed. You cannot be a stowaway if you are not stowed.'

Bunny called them over to where Uma had been working. 'Uma will show you chaps how to drive these things. They are only built for one person and one robot, so it's lucky you don't eat too much naan.'

Without any apparent effort, Uma picked up a robot and used Velcro to secure it behind a seat on the LRV.

'Driving this is a piece of cake,' she began. 'And driving here is gonna be *da bomb!*'

9

Uma was right. Cruising across the lunar landscape was exhilarating. Dev steered clear of big craters, but he also looked out for the small ones—so that he could drive straight through them.

'Whoa!' OP shouted, hanging on for dear life as they flew over the lip of a four-metre bowl.

Dev whooped as they landed on the moon for the second time that day. 'How often do you get a chance to do that?'

'The lunar speed record is only 18 kilometres per hour, so you've already smashed it. If you kill us now, we don't get to tell anyone about it.'

'Do you know what's great about this? There's no traffic.'

'Just wait till it's the mining capital of the universe,' OP replied. 'There's more than lithium up here, you know. There's helium-3, and that can create nuclear power without radioactive waste.'

'Wait,' Dev said. 'Can you hear that?'

Something in the LRV was rattling. It wasn't a small rattle. In fact, it was more of a clattering noise. Dev slowed to a halt and they got down to inspect the vehicle.

'What's that?'

Crouched near the front of the LRV, Dev was pointing to the wheel assembly. A kind of stick had got lodged in it, and the end had been mangled while they were in motion. Dev reached for it.

It was light, but it was metal and far too corroded to have come off the LRV.

'Space junk?' Dev wondered.

OP was lost in thought. He tried to scratch his chin, only to remember he was wearing a space helmet and gloves.

'Definitely. Yes, it's space junk. But I don't think it just fell here. It was put here.'

'Why do you think that?'

'It's some kind of aluminium. And look, it's telescopic. This bit once slid into that bit, though now it's stuck in one place . . . It might be . . . Well, the Americans like to leave flags here, even though they start fading the moment they leave. I'm ninety nine point nine per cent sure that this is one of their flagpoles.'

'And they talk about the litter in India,' Dev said. 'Next, we'll be finding one of their golf balls.'

OP unzipped one of the compartments on his spacesuit and reached inside. He held a glove out towards Dev, palm down before swivelling his wrist and opening his hand. The object inside was grey and weathered, but unmistakably meant for a place much greener than the moon.

'I wasn't going to tell you just yet . . .' OP confessed. 'I trod on it when we landed.'

'Come on, let's set our robot free and get back to the ship.'

10

'**S**ir, I have a question for you,' Dev said.

Bunny was playing a game on his phone as they hurtled towards Earth. 'I'm all ears.'

Typical adult, thought Dev. *That's what Amma says when she's actually posting something to Facebook.*

'How old are you?'

'Well, some people think that's a rude question, but I don't mind. Thirty-nine.'

'A-ha!' OP exclaimed.

Dev smiled. 'How about you, Venky?'

'He's an old chap. Forty,' Bunny cut in.

'But Rinny and Uma must be younger, right?'

'Don't tell anyone,' Bunny said loudly, 'but Rinny is actually older.' Having caught Rinny's attention, he dropped his voice again. 'She looks young, but she's forty-four.'

Rinny tossed back her hair. 'I look like a girr, right?'

Dev could tell that OP was calculating averages. He looked inquiringly at Uma.

'I'm the baby of the crew, just out of my teens.'

'She's thirty-three,' Bunny said.

OP's brain ticked fast.

Dev's ticked too, a tad or three slower.

'So that is . . .'

Why did it take him so long to work out simple maths problems? Baba was always scolding him for this, though even he kept his trusty calculator within reach.

'So that is . . .' Dev closed his eyes, concentrating hard. 'One hundred and fifty s-six . . . divided by four . . .'

'Yes, Dev?'

Mrs Kaur was standing in front of his desk.

'Yes?'

'Thirty-nine?'

'Very good, Dev. And there I was, thinking you might be daydreaming again.'

'Oh no, ma'am. I've learnt my lesson, ma'am. The present is a gift, ma'am. You won't find me drifting off into space . . .'

Acknowledgements

I want to thank thousands of people—so that is exactly what I'm going to do. Between October and December 2019, and again in February 2020, I presented sessions to thousands of children in Delhi, Chennai, Kolkata, Mumbai and Varanasi. Audiences embraced me and loved Daydreamer Dev's adventures climbing Everest, tracing the Amazon and crossing the Sahara. They wanted more! Being a sensible man—something those audiences would probably dispute—I took the opportunity of asking where Daydreamer Dev should take off to next. The places we go in this volume are the children's top choices. Thank you, girls and boys! I promise that I'll be back as soon as I possibly can to see how you enjoyed these stories, and I'll ask the same question again.

Some slightly older but equally awesome people I must thank are Puffin's Sohini Mitra, a woman of action and a real gem of an editor; Shalini Agrawal, whose attention to detail is phenomenal; and Antra K, the super-talented designer. I feel fortunate to be working with the best, and that also applies to our illustrator, Suvidha Mistry. The diverse characters and settings in my stories added up to a challenging assignment, and the work you've done is superb. Don't you agree, folks?

The Absolutely True Adventures of Daydreamer Dev: Volume 1

Ken Spillman

Chronicling three of Daydreamer Dev's fantastic adventures

Sitting in class or watching clouds from the roof of Kwality Carpets, Dev's flights of fancy land him in challenging environments all over the globe. Baba says that if there were medals for daydreaming, Dev would be an All-India Champion—maybe even an Olympic hero.

These action-packed stories transport the reader to three iconic locations:

*Follow Dev as he accompanies the ghost of a Sherpa woman on a quest to conquer **Mount Everest**. Ride with Dev as he traces the **Amazon River**, which proves much more difficult than going with the flow! Join Dev and his pal OP as they set out from Timbuktu to cross the **Sahara** on malodorous camels.*

For Dev and his colourful imagination, it's Access All Areas and No Holds Barred.

Friends Behind Walls

Harshikaa Udasi

Why won't anyone let Inu and Putti be friends?

Putti is spending his summer vacation in Deolali and he thinks life is going to be fun with his new friend Inu. But with their parents FORBIDDING them from playing with each other, the two kids are flabbergasted. Flab-ber-gas-ted. Means shocked. Nothing to do with food and farts.

Now the two of them have decided to find out why. Can Mr Om Namaha and Dr Solanki help? Or will I and P have to go up the hill to the fearsome Tekdichi Mhatari to solve this mystery?